MENAGE SEX TALES

EXPLICIT DIRTY EROTICA SHORT STORIES

KELLEN PRIME

plicit Press

CHAPTER 1

WILD ONE

PRINCESS KATHERINE OF SHADA crept through the shadows after her older sister. In her plain cotton dress and a gray cloak covering her heavy bittersweet waves, the seventeen-year-old blended in with the commoners. She kept her dark green eyes on the petite figure in front of her, the dark blue conspicuous among the more muted colors of the rest of the crowd. At eighteen, Valeria was free to come and go. She didn't need to hide who she was. As for where she was going, Kat intended to see for herself.

Valeria was, outwardly at least, everything a princess should be. She had perfectly coifed blonde hair and pale blue eyes. Always neat and clean, on time and never disappearing to the stables because the company of horses was preferred to that of people. But over the last year, Kat had begun to suspect that Valeria wasn't as perfect as she seemed, at least in one particular area.

Every Shadan royal or noble was trained in the art of love-making starting at the age of sixteen.

. . .

This culminated with the loss of virginity during their seventeenth year. After their first encounter, sexuality wasn't restricted, but the higher the nobility, the more closely the chosen partners were scrutinized. Multiple encounters were discouraged, if for no other reason than to ensure there were no romantic entanglements. Arranged marriages were commonplace and monogamy was expected afterward, so every Shadan royal and noble youth had it drilled into their heads that they could fuck all they wanted as long as they didn't fall in love.

From what Kat had heard, her sister didn't have a problem with the not falling in love aspect of Shadan rule but did have a proclivity for choosing partners who weren't exactly appropriate and meeting them multiple times. It was this rumor that had drawn Kat out of her usual solitude to follow Valeria into the village. Tomorrow, Kat would begin the physical aspect of her training and her stomach had been in knots thinking about what she would be doing with her assigned partner, Petyr, a nice enough son of a duke that she'd met once or twice. Everything she'd learned so far had been theory and pictures. If Valeria was doing what the rumors said, Kat could be able to see for herself what was going to happen to her.

Valeria turned down a narrow passage and disappeared through a nearly hidden door. Kat paused just outside, peering through the crack at what was happening inside.

"You started without me," Valeria tossed aside her cloak.

The two young men on the floor looked up from where they were lying, skin glistening with sweat. Enoi, the black-smith's apprentice, had dark brown hair and unique amber eyes. His tall frame was heavily muscled. He had calluses on his large hands and his tanned skin was marked with burns. He was underneath Jal, a farmer's son with white-blond hair and dark chocolate eyes. Though similarly tanned from being outdoors, Jal's frame was leaner than Enoi's. The smaller man was stretched out on Enoi, their hard lengths swollen as they rubbed against each other.

"You're late," Enoi grinned. He ran his large hands down Jal's back to grip the farmer's firm ass.

Valeria rolled her pale eyes as she crossed to the table that stood against one wall. She hopped up on it and pulled the skirt of the gown up around her waist, revealing her lack of undergarments. "My parents are expecting me back for dinner."

Jal rolled off of the larger man, hand dropping to his thick shaft. He stroked it as he walked towards Valeria, eyes darkened to near black. Enoi stood as well, hand running over his hard flesh as he watched. Valeria's eyes glowed with the possessive light of a woman who knew what was going to happen because it had happened before. She reached down between her legs, fingers brushing over the thin layer of pale hair to slip between her folds. She dipped her finger inside and when she withdrew it, the digit glistened with her juices. She held out her hand and Jal took the pro-offered finger into his mouth, sucking it clean.

Enoi's arm slid around Jal's waist, his hand dropping to wrap around the younger man's cock. Jal's hips jerked, head falling back as Valeria's finger slipped from his mouth. Valeria's eyes met Enoi's over Jal's shoulder, reading her own lust in his eyes. Enoi forced Jal forward until the young man's cock bumped against Valeria's entrance.

. . .

"Yes," she hissed. Her heels brushed against Enoi's hips. Her back arched as Jal slid inside, each inch stretching her, sending little sparks of pleasure through her body.

He leaned over her, covering her mouth with his as his pelvis came to rest against her, his length fully sheathed in her wet heat. His tongue teased at the seam of her lips and she opened to him, swallowing his gasps as Enoi pushed one spit-slicked finger into his ass. Jal's entire body twitched as Enoi began to pump his finger, twisting and stretching.

"Just do it," Jal ripped his mouth from Valeria's, his voice trembling nearly as much as the muscles in his arms.

"Just remember you asked me to," Enoi warned. He removed his finger and spit in his hand, fisting his cock to spread the liquid. "No complaints."

Jal shook his head and turned his attention back to Valeria's mouth. His lips slanted over hers, tongue thrusting into the moist cavern. He moaned as Enoi pressed the blunt head against his hole, the sound turning to a pained noise as it pushed past the ring of protesting muscle. Valeria sucked on Jal's tongue, hands running over the farmer's chest, scraping her nails over his flat nipples, each touch helping to each the burn in the young man's ass.

When Enoi's balls were resting against Jal's cheeks, he reached one large hand around to stroke the little bundle of nerves between Valeria's legs. She keened, the cries muffled by Jal's mouth, the sound spurring Enoi on. They began to move, Enoi pulling back enough to allow Jal to do the same before the apprentice snapped his hips forward, burying himself in Jal's ass and forcing the younger man's cock deep inside the princess.

Kat swallowed hard as she watched the two men

fucking each other and her sister. She'd known, intellectu-
ally of course, that some people preferred partners of the
same sex and some liked both. She'd just never realized how
these things could work together to elicit the cries of pleasure she was hearing from the trio inside. Her eyes had
widened in amazement when she'd seen the impressive
length disappearing into her sister's cunt and she hadn't
been able to stop her gasp when the dark-haired man had
pushed what looked like at least nine inches into the other
man's ass. Then, as they began to move, she felt herself grow
wet, desire coiling low in her belly. When the men's bodies
had stiffened, their thrusts erratic, she'd known that they'd
found their release and her eyes had darted to her sister's
face, needing to know if it had been mutual.

The expression on the princess's face had been one of
total ecstasy and Kat instantly knew that the rumors about
her sister were true. Before any of the trio disentangled
themselves, she pulled her cloak tighter around her and
headed back to the castle. After all, she needed her rest. If
that was what she had to look forward to, she had a feeling
she was going to enjoy the rest of her training.

CHAPTER 2

WORKING UP A SWEAT

JOLEEN NAIRN LOVED COMING to the gym with her boyfriend. At least, that's what the twenty-one-year-old told herself as she followed twenty-year-old Izzak Kitzinger inside. She'd been sound asleep when Izzak had come home from the late shift at the factory where he worked. When he'd woken her, he hadn't explained why they were going to the gym at two in the morning, but he'd had that look in his olive eyes, the look that said she was going to do as she was told and that it would be worth it.

She'd run a hand through her short corn silk waves, splashed some water on her face, and waited for Izzak to tell her what to wear. When he just handed her his overcoat, she'd shivered with anticipation. She'd watched him the entire way to the gym, wanting to run her fingers through his thick bronze hair, over his sculpted chest. Izzak was gorgeous in that insanely fuckable way that drove straight women and gay men crazy.

And speaking of men...

. . .

As soon as she saw the man on the rowing machine, she knew why Izzak had brought them here. They'd been discussing a threesome for weeks and Izzak had been hinting that someone they knew would be the third party. Joleen had assumed, wrongly it seemed, that Izzak had been referring to a woman. She would have done it if Izzak had told her to, but she'd been secretly hoping for another man. Blane St. Matthews was a twenty-five-year-old stockbroker that Izzak and she had both talked to over the past few weeks. With hair the color of caramel, cat green eyes, and a tall, lean body that most athletes would envy, Blane was exactly who she would've wanted to be their third.

"Izzak, Joleen," Blane had a look of genuine confusion on his face and Joleen shook her head.

Leave it to Izzak to surprise everyone. "What are you guys doing here so late?"

"I would say that it was because I just got off the late shift and we wanted to work out, but that'd be a lie," Izzak grinned as he sat on the weight bench.

Curiosity replaced confusion. "Then why?"

Izzak didn't take his eyes off of Blane, wanting to see the older man's face. "Joleen."

He only had to say her name and she knew what he wanted. She untied the overcoat she was wearing and dropped it from her shoulders in one smooth motion. Like Izzak, she watched Blane's eyes widen, then darken in appreciation. A hot flush ran over Joleen's body but she didn't protest or move to cover herself. She was still wearing what she'd slept in: a tiny pair of pink shorts that were short enough to almost be underwear and a white camisole, both of which were about a size too small. In fact, her breasts were nearly spilling over the top of her shirt.

"What's going on?" Blane couldn't take his eyes off of Joleen's voluptuous body. "What's going on is that I want you to fuck Joleen while she gives me a blow job," Izzak

chuckled at the shocked expression on Blane's face.

After a moment, he spoke again, his voice pitched low, turning into that liquid sex sound that could make Joleen wet with a single word. What he said next sent such a flood of juices to her pussy that she knew her shorts were soaking through.

"I've seen you watching her, Blane. It's all right. I can't blame you. Who wouldn't want to see those 40 E tits when she runs? Or watch that tight ass and think about what it must be like to be buried inside? I can tell you this, her pussy is still as tight as the day I popped her cherry. And her ass? Shit, I love spanking her until her cheeks are red and then making her sit on me. She sure bounces fast when her cheeks burn, even with all eight inches up her ass."

Joleen felt the desire that had been simmering in her belly bubble up, washing over her body until she wanted to squirm, but she knew better. If she moved before Izzak told her to, he'd punish her. Tonight was a reward. She didn't want to spoil it.

Izzak didn't wait for Blane to respond, which was probably a good thing since the other man appeared to be having difficulties putting words into sentences. Rather, Izzak snapped his fingers, signaling for Joleen to move. She knew every command by heart and immediately complied. She crossed to where Izzak was sitting and turned to face him. He pulled down the front of her camisole, eyes darkening as her breasts were freed, but he didn't touch her. He nodded and she got down on all fours. By the time she'd arranged herself, she knew Blane was kneeling behind her.

"Are you sure about this?"

Izzak reached into his pocket and tossed a foil packet over Joleen. Blane caught it and Joleen heard the sound of the packet tearing.

"You should see his cock, Jo," Izzak pulled his sweatpants down on his hips just far enough to free his own hard length. "Damn, it's got to be ten inches."

"Eleven."

The couple could hear the note of pride in Blane's voice.

"Don't worry about foreplay," Izzak lazily began to stroke his shaft. "She's been soaking since we walked in."

Joleen shuddered as she felt an unfamiliar hand between her legs, ghosting over the wet crotch of her shorts. She kept her eyes on Izzak, body shivering in anticipation. Blane's hands moved to her hips, fingers hooking under her waistband. A cool breeze caressed her overheated skin as Blane exposed it, lowering her shorts to her knees.

"Fuck," Blane swore as his tip pushed past her entrance. "You weren't kidding."

. . .

As he worked his way inside, each inch sent a ripple of pleasure through Joleen, forcing her to bite her bottom lip to keep from crying out. When his balls finally came to rest on her ass, every muscle in her body was trembling with the effort of stopping herself from cumming. Izzak's hand on her head gave her a momentary distraction from the slow, deep strokes Blane was currently making.

"You're going to swallow like a good girl, right?"

Joleen knew the question was rhetorical. She opened her mouth as Izzak guided her to his swollen cock. She could always judge how close he was by how fast he made her start. If he just placed her lips on the tip, he wanted something slow and leisurely. The fact that he pushed himself straight into her mouth meant he wasn't going to last long. Judging by the increased pace at which Blane was now pounding into her, she had a feeling he was on the same page.

Each thrust pushed her forward so she let the natural momentum work in her favor. Izzak's fingers flexed on her head, but he let her be in control. As she worked her way up to his shaft, she increased suction, then let every slide down put him further and further into her mouth. She could feel pressure building low in her belly as Blane's cock kept up its delicious friction and fought to concentrate on the dick in her mouth.

"Don't you dare," Izzak somehow still managed to

convey authority in a breathless voice. "You are not allowed to cum until I tell you."

Joleen blinked to show that she heard him and tried to focus on the feel of him, the weight of him on her tongue. His taste, salty and something darkly spicy, was uniquely him.

"Fuck, I'm going to cum," Blane's fingers dug into her hips.

Joleen took a deep breath and relaxed her throat, letting Blane's final forceful thrust shove her forward onto Izzak's cock. She heard Izzak call out her name as his dick slipped down her throat and she swallowed, the muscles in her throat massaging the end of his shaft until he exploded. She lifted her head, letting his cum coat her tongue as his cock fell from her mouth. At the same time, she felt Blane pull out, leaving her pussy aching for relief.

"Did you cum?" Izzak asked.

Joleen shook her head, whimpering as Blane's hands cupped her breasts. Izzak slid off the bench and pressed his lips to hers, an oddly chaste kiss. "Don't worry," he whispered. "Eventually, we'll take care of you." He looked over her head at Blane. "Up for round two?"

CHAPTER 3

THE STAR COLLISION

TWENTY-TWO-YEAR-OLD CARLYE MCGOVERN had wanted to come to Comic-Con since she was a kid. So, when she'd caught the asshole she'd been dating in bed with her best friend the night before they'd been scheduled to fly to LA, she hadn't thought twice about going without him. But that didn't matter now. No, what mattered was the VIP pass and the reservation at the nicest hotel in the city currently clutched in her hand.

After a quick nap, a bite to eat, and a shower, Carlye was ready to go. Her slate-blue eyes were wide with excitement and her long champagne-colored hair was pinned up behind her head. Wearing jeans and a t-shirt, she looked more like a fresh-faced teenager than a newly graduated paralegal. So entranced with her surroundings was she that she ran smack-dab into a wall of muscle before she even realized anyone was there.

"Oh! I'm so sorry," she was stammering an apology before she even saw who she'd collided with. When recognition did set in, her words dried up and she simply stared.

Six feet, five-inch Riah Kasey had stylishly tousled

tawny hair, heart-stopping cobalt eyes, and one of the most gorgeous faces and hottest bodies on television. At twenty-three, he and his childhood best friend, twenty-five-year-old Kent Chilton had the best rags-to-riches story in Holly-wood. They not only starred in TV's biggest new show as fallen angels competing for the same girl but were also the show's creators and head writers. Riah played the sensitive, charming 'good' angel Raziel, while Kent was the dark and brooding Samael. With his dark red hair and slate gray eyes, Kent was easily striking as his friend. At only six foot two, he was shorter, his build more lean and chiseled, his face more angular and fierce. One of Carlye's friends had once commented that Kent had an expression that said he wanted to do bad things to his fans and knew that they'd let him. And they'd like it.

And he was giving her that look right now, his weighted gaze running over her body. "Hi," Riah grinned. "I'm Riah, this is Kent."

"Carlye," she found her voice but couldn't stop staring.

"So, Carlye, want to get some coffee with us? We've got a couple hours to kill before the first

panel."

"Coffee?"

"Unless there's something else you can think of that we could do for a few hours?" Riah's eyes darkened and he took a step forward.

"I can," Kent made the two words sound far more decadent than any words had the right to.

Less than fifteen minutes later, Carlye found herself following her two biggest celebrity crushes into a hotel room, still not quite certain how this was happening. Then, as soon as the door closed, their hands were on her and she stopped caring.

Kent's movements were deliberate, every place his fingers touched made Carlye's skin burned, and a deep smolder slowly spread through her body. He peeled off her t-shirt as Riah dropped to his knees to work on her jeans. A cool breeze caressed her bare breasts and she resisted the urge to cover herself. Riah's' touch was different than his friend's, firm strokes designed to send electricity racing across her nerves. When he pressed his lips to the sensitive skin just below her belly button, Carlye shivered. Kent pulled the pins from her hair, sending the silky strands tumbling down her back. He placed an open-mouthed kiss on the side of her neck, sliding his hands up her ribcage to cup Carlye's small breasts and her head fell back against his shoulder. Riah yanked down Carlye's pants, running his tongue up the inside of her thigh as he lifted her legs. He hooked her knees over his shoulders and tossed her jeans aside.

The men shifted together, their movements a dance as they positioned Carlye exactly how they wanted her. Kent took her weight on his chest, his heart slow and steady against her back, his skin hot. She didn't remember him removing his shirt. Riah moved closer, her legs sliding down his back until his face was just a centimeter away from the crotch of her teal panties. He wrapped his hands up around her thighs and ran his nose along her slit.

"He's going to slide his tongue deep inside you," Kent's low voice broke the silence. "It's sinfully long, can reach places that you've never dreamed."

Carlye whimpered as Riah pulled aside her panties and did exactly as Kent said, the thick muscle swiftly breaching her entrance to work its way into her throbbing cunt. As Riah proved that his talents were not limited to acting and writing, Kent disproved the commonly held notion that he was the quiet one.

"He'd very good, isn't he? I'll bet you're creaming as he caresses those silken walls, feeling your pussy muscles quivering around him. Any moment now, he's going to move up to your clit, suck that little nub into his mouth and make you scream."

Carlye caught her breath as Riah's mouth followed Kent's directions. That's what they were, she realized now. They had a system, a routine. These two famous men that she and thousands, if not millions of women had fantasized about, were accustomed to sharing women. The thought turned her on so much that the instant Riah's lips closed around her clit, she came, crying out her pleasure as her body shook.

"That wasn't nearly loud enough," Kent's fingers danced over her skin, trailing down her stomach to where Riah's head moved between her legs. There, his hands briefly left her body and she felt Riah's head drop lower. Carlye forced her eyes open and watched Kent's fingers rake through Riah's hair.

This is so fucking hot. The thought raced through her

mind... then disappeared as Riah's tongue was suddenly someplace new. She made a strangled sound that might have been a protest if Kent hadn't chosen that moment to return his hands to her breasts, thumb, and forefinger rolling her nipples into hardpoints.

"He's going to work his tongue into your asshole now," Kent's lips were at her ear, hot air puffing against her skin with every word. "Trust me; you're going to want him to do this. In a second, he's going to put his finger in your pussy to keep you nice and wet."

Carlye's back arched as Riah's finger penetrated her, hips involuntarily jerking. The tip of his tongue pushed past the ring of muscle and she shuddered. This couldn't be happening, could it? Was she really being held by Kent Chilton while Riah Kasey finger fucked her pussy and licked her ass? Things like this didn't happen to her.

"Once we've got you stretched out, things are going to go fast the first time," Kent's teeth scraped over the shell of her ear and Carlye swore. "It's been too long since either of us has fucked." He pushed his hips against her back and she felt the hard length of him against the top of her ass. "But we've both got good recovery time. Plenty of time to go again and again before we have to leave."

Riah's finger slipped from her pussy and Carlye started to protest but tensed as the tip circled the area where Riah's tongue had just been.

"Shh," Kent slid a hand down over her stomach to dip between her folds. "Riah's going to put his finger in your ass and you're going to cum again." He began to make circular motions over her clit as Riah did as he was told.

Carlye hissed, and then came as Kent's fingers worked their magic. She barely noticed Riah stretching her, sliding in a second finger, scissoring them. Each sensation just rolled her body from one orgasm into the next. It wasn't until Riah stood that she was aware that something else was about to happen.

"We're only going to get in a few strokes before we cum," Kent had a hand at his waist. "And you're going to scream this time."

She heard the sound of ripping foil and had a moment to think *holy shit they're both going to fuck me* before she felt the tip of Riah's cock at her entrance. She wailed as he buried himself in one thrust, stretching her too wide, too fast, but it was just right and just enough and she was cumming again if she'd ever stopped. Her limbs went limp as he fucked up into her once, twice before stilling, every muscle in his body tensing as he fought to keep control. It took her a moment to realize why, but her body was still humming and she couldn't have moved if she'd wanted to.

"I'm going to fuck your pretty little ass now," Kent whispered. "We're only going to do it for a few seconds together before Riah cums. I won't be far behind, but it'll be enough for you to get another one. I want you to scream loud enough for the entire floor to hear."

When he shoved his cock into her ass, Carlye did just that, back arching and body convulsing with excess stimulation. She couldn't believe that anyone could feel so much, that pain could turn into such intense pleasure. Then everything was going gray and she was falling forward even as Riah cried out her name.

By the time the trio left the room to head down to their first panel, Carlye was surprised that she could even walk, and, judging by the self-satisfied smirks both men were wearing, they'd enjoyed themselves just as much. Her suspicions were confirmed when; just before they parted ways – her to the audience, them to the stage – Kent leaned down and asked her if she wanted to meet them afterward. She didn't hesitate, didn't think about how sore she'd be the next day. She'd simply smiled and said 'yes.'

This was definitely going to be a week she'd never forget.

CHAPTER 4

KAMA SUTRA: THE ORGY PARTY

THERE I WAS, being fucked in my ass by Ted, while Jim twirled and sucked my nipples, and I was licking Justin's enormous penis. It was an orgy and there were 12 of us with our own partners, who freely interacted with the others.

It was our high school reunion. My husband Tim and I were invited. I was excited about it because I'll be meeting again my first love, Matthew.

We were all naked, and having the dream orgy of our lives.

Matthew found me first, and I was visibly happy; his dick was as big as a horse's. He got married to my best friend Sylvia and I cried over that for several weeks. Now, Matt was standing before me, his body chiseled like a Greek god, his penis paying homage to me, as Ted and Justin deliciously explored my tits and ass.

Matt approached and wrestled me from Jim, as he brought down his lips to devour my own. "I've missed you," he hissed into my ear as he lifted my left thigh and thrust his dick into my eagerly waiting vagina.

Ted pulled me down to sit on his lap as he refused to detach himself from my tight quivering ass.

This made Matt lean towards me as he thrust in and out of my wet pussy. We were on the couch, with Ted below me, fucking my ass, and Matt above fucking my pussy. Jim continued to lick my tits in between Matt's and Ted's increasing pace.

Matt stopped thrusting and lay prone on top of me. He began rocking up and down his groin increasing the pressure on my clitoris and my pubis. This made me wild with desire.

Then the other women appeared and everyone was touching the skin all over my body, exploring whatever exposed flesh I have left open.

I went mad with joy, as hands touched and sucked all my erotic zones and I grabbed at someone's breast too as Matt jammed his cock into my pussy and roared with his nearing orgasm. Ted, under me, was also nearing his climax.

All hands were on the three of us, urging us to go on. My husband stooped to French kiss me and draw my tongue into his own. I felt my climax surfacing on the horizon of my consciousness. Matt came with a shudder and Ted came as well, both men pinning me between them, as they both locked their dicks into my ass and pussy.

I was on the verge of my orgasm too, and I was frantically straining my crotch to achieve it. As soon as Matt and Ted disengaged themselves from me, the others replaced them. They did not leave though but continued to fondle my tits and pussy.

Leo towered over me as Bessie played with his balls. I could see that he was aroused by the way my body was clamoring for fulfillment; I was on the verge of exploding.

He raised my arms high above my head and spread my legs wide apart as Bessie and the other girls were continuously caressing my thighs, fondling my tits, and Tim continued sucking my lips and tongue.

Leo carried me onto the floor and pulled a pillow under my buttocks that lifted my groin higher towards him. His eyes almost bulged with excitement as he planted his hands on each of my side and plunged his hot rod into my warm pussy.

I moaned delightedly as he moved inside me in a languid, titillating movement that intensified my arousal. I was breathless with the sheer ecstasy of it all. *Oh, god, this is unbelievable*, I thought. The friction of his pubis against my own stimulated my clit and it gave me ecstasy beyond description.

Then the whole party was all over us again. I felt hands stroking my tingling breasts, tongues sucking my lips, fingers fondling my clit, fingers fucking my ass, and seeking tongues and hot fingers all around my body.

It was utter bliss. The multiple varied sensations assailing my body were giving me a once-in-a-lifetime experience that left me gasping and crying in delight.

Then I felt myself quiver as every fiber in my body became ablaze with tingling, encompassing delightful pleasures. They left me writhing uncontrollably and screaming my lungs out as rolls and rolls of mundane pleasures inundated my body. It was an orgasm I have never experienced in my lifetime.

After I have climaxed, someone started sucking my clit

again, and there was a hard dick shoved into my mouth. Oh, god, the pleasure never ceased to build again.

I thought I was already satiated but the urgent tongue exploring my pussy was arousing me anew. I returned the favor by savoring the penis before my face. I fondled his balls and ran my tongue up and down his shaft until his dick became even larger and distended.

A second dick was thrust into my mouth and I alternated sucking and running my tongue between the two dicks. They were both long and thick that I almost choked when they both thrust them into my sex-hungry mouth.

I felt hands and tongues all over my body again. I was seated on the couch while someone was seated on the floor discovering the hidden recesses of my vagina with his tongue and fingers. The two men were standing on the couch on each of my sides and my head was turned right and left to respond to their growing sexual needs.

I can't complain though, because the pleasure I was feeling was beyond measure. My pussy was again tightening for a nearing orgasm. I sucked relentlessly on the two dicks, my tongue coming out now and then, to lick the tips of their dicks.

I fondled their balls as well, as I twirled them playfully around my fingers, and drop a kiss now and then to the skin between them. The tongue in my pussy moved faster.

I moaned as three fingers went inside my slick pussy, and the tongue continued to draw delight from my clit. A mouth was on my tits alternately sucking and licking them, making me shiver with joy. Oh god, I was coming again.

I no longer was aware of who was creating the sensations in my body. My body was jerking and twitching wantonly as I saw a blinding, flash of light, and my orgasm inundated my body over and over again; each one more powerful than the previous sensation.

I lay there spent but happy and satiated as other another dick entered my pussy again in another position. I started to come alive again, and my pussy responded with enthusiasm.

It was the ultimate Kama Sutra!

CHAPTER 5

SEEKING OUT COUPLE'S THERAPY

MAX AND DIANNE had been having some trouble for a while. Dianne had no idea what she was going to do. It seemed that twenty years of marriage had finally got Max to the point that he was seeking out fresh younger women that whom he was able to have sex with and still feel like a young man. At only forty-one years old, Max had felt for a while that his life had passed him by and that he was not a young stud anymore. Dianne, on the other hand, still felt that she was a smoking hot woman even though she was forty-three. Dianne had tried everything under the sun that she could to keep Max interested in her.

She bought outfits that were a little on the risqué side as well as trying new positions. She had damn near gone through the entire Kama Sutra in an attempt to spice things up in the bedroom. Nothing seemed to work. Dianne was in her yard one day when she saw her neighbor Gina sunbathing naked. Gina had the type of body that any man would go for. She had perky breasts a nice figure and a shaved bush. Gina was never alone for long. It was common for Dianne to go to the kitchen, look out the window and see Gina in her house having wild sex. That was the bad part of the way their houses sat. The kitchen window allowed a perfect view into Gina's house. This meant that if her blinds were open you were able to stand in the kitchen and watch Gina and her male companion fuck their brains out. Dianne had caught Max watching on a number of different occasions.

Dianne decided to head over to Gina's house and talk to her to see if the younger female had any ideas that she was able to give Dianne. Gina seemed to be the best source of information, as she was a woman that Max desired, and deep down, Dianne was not opposed to the thought of her and Gina getting together and having some fun.

"How do you do it, Gina, I mean you have men falling over themselves to get with you. There are nights I have caught Max masturbating while you have sex in your bedroom."

"Look, the secret to great sex is for you to be out there and do things that make you feel young. From what you have told me, you have tried new positions and new clothing. One area that may help is to try new experiences. Try bringing a third woman in or even try doing it in public places where you may be caught." Gina said as she got up to go and make her and Dianne a couple of drinks. Gina loved to drink and that was one thing that seemed to get her laid more than anything else. Gina would go and get drunk and then simply sleep with the first dick that came along. There were times that Gina had more than one man pounding her at any given time. There was one night that Dianne remembered that involved Gina being fucked in the pussy, mouth, and ass by three men all at the same time.

After a couple of hours, Dianne had one too many drinks and was in no shape to head home alone. Gina decided to help Dianne home and at least help her get into bed before Max got home. Gina got her to the bedroom. As she was helping Dianne over to the bed, Dianne turned around and planted a giant kiss on Gina's lips while getting a feel of Gina's large breasts. Dianne then passed out on her back on the bed with her top half unbuttoned. Gina stood there and had to wonder what she should do about the situation. Gina was an equal opportunity giver of sex; male or female it made no difference to her.

Gina knew that deep down it was not right for her to take advantage of the situation but then again Dianne was laying there with her body all but inviting her to go ahead. She also knew that Max was due to be home at any moment and did not want to be caught with Dianne by Max. Before Gina had the chance to do anything, she heard the door open and saw Max walking into the house. Gina was paralyzed, as she knew that things did not look good. Max walked to the bedroom and found his wife passed out with Gina in the room.

"Wow, you two couldn't wait till I arrived? Hell, I would have loved the show, sorry I missed it."

"Max, me, and Dianne have not done anything. She got a little drunk at my house, I brought her home she kissed me, felt me up, and then passed out like this."

Max responded to this and looked at Gina. "We're here. She is passed out and will never know the difference, besides if she does come too it will give her something to watch while the alcohol wears off. I say that we go into the kitchen and get it on."

Gina and Max made their way to the kitchen, as Gina was not going to turn down the chance to fuck. She had heard that he had a large cock and she needed a man to give her a good tit fucking. Gina removed her top and pulled her bra down to allow Max full access to her DD tits. Max made quick work of his clothes and made his way over to where Gina was leaning on a counter and began to suck on Gina's tits. While he did this, Max took one of his free hands and slipped it up under her skirt and began to finger her dripping wet pussy. Gina almost became butter in Max's hands as he was playing her pussy like a well-tuned instrument. Max pulled himself closer to Gina and took his hand out from under her skirt and replaced it with his now rock hard 13" cock.

Gina suggested that they head back to the bedroom where Dianne was so she could enjoy the show. Max carried her into the room and placed her on the bed beside Dianne. Max mounted up onto Gina and slid his cock back into her warm, wet hole. It had been a few months since he last cheated on Dianne and he had forgotten what a tight, young pussy felt like. While Gina was being fucked hard, Dianne suddenly woke up and straddled Gina's face. Dianne seemed to get sober very quick. Gina found out that the two of them had played Gina. It was arranged for all of this to happen. Gina was now in the position of being fucked by Max while in the position of eating out Dianne's pussy. Gina could not believe that she had allowed herself to become such a part of the therapy of Dianne and Max trying to save their marriage.

CHAPTER 6

THE LUST OF MÉNAGE

MY HUSBAND and I had been looking for new ways to spice up our 10-year marriage that had been going stale in the sex department lately. We had discussed various options and finally decided on one. I ran an ad online for a hot, sexy lady to come and share our love bed for a lusty ménage.

We got some replies to our ad and we finally agreed on a pretty brunette that had sent us photos of herself. She was about 25 with long, straight dark hair and blue eyes. The best thing about her was her hot body. She was petite with perky tits and a nice round ass. She had also shown us pictures of her pussy, which was exactly how my husband liked them. It wasn't too furry but it wasn't bald either.

I got some beers in the freezer chilling and put on some old rock 'n roll tunes in preparation for Candice to arrive. She had given us her first name. She seemed very friendly and we were both anxious for her to arrive. Finally, we heard her knock at the door, and my hubby and I looked at each other and he nodded for me to answer the door. I swung the door open and I was pleased with what I saw immediately. My husband seemed equally as pleased.

Candice was perfect for what we were looking for. She had a girl-next-door appearance and a smile that lit up the room.

I took Candice's coat and led her into our den where she sat down on the sofa. I offered her a beer and scampered to the kitchen to grab 3 for us. We chatted for a while, getting to know one another, and then we started to loosen up a bit. Candice then removed her shirt without any warning, revealing to us her perky, pink buds. I was a bit surprised she was getting naughty so quickly, but happily surprised that's for sure! I gave hubby a look as if to say, "come over here and let's suck these beautiful breasts" so hubby did as I had signaled him to.

I took the right tit and hubby took care of her left one. We both started doing our own thing on Candice's hot tits. She moaned like a giddy schoolgirl telling us she enjoyed the sucking and licking of her nipples. She stood up slowly and wiggled out of her chinos revealing a beautiful body underneath. I could tell hubby was getting a hard-on by the way he was grabbing for his crotch inadvertently. So I nodded to him and he and I both started peeling our clothes off.

Candice had her fingers inside her wet snatch watching him and I get unclothed and in the nude for her. She walked over to us and she took my right ample tit in her mouth. I loved having my huge tits sucked almost more than anything, and Candice was a natural. She took her right hand and while she suckled my horny tits, she stroked hubby's long erection up and down his rock-hard shaft. Hubby took the liberty of fingering her and me off. We were all getting some action by this point in our naughty ménage.

We eventually took our ménage action to the bedroom.

We all three got onto the bed and managed to get into a very kinky position. At first, Candice and I laid side by side for hubby to see the full view of our beautiful female bodies. He put one hand in her cunt and the other in mine and started fingering the fuck out of us. As he fingered us, he'd plunge his needy cock into our mouths one at a time flipping back and forth between the two. It was very exciting not knowing when he'd yank his stiff dick out and give it to the other girl. He also took turns wallowing in our nasty cunts. He started with mine, got me almost to the point of orgasm, and then buried his head between Candice's thighs. She loved the way my hubby ate her out because she started to nearly scream when his mouth latched onto her clit. While he ate her off, I sucked the fuck out of his greedy cock. He had always loved how I gave him a blowjob. He pushed his cock back harder down my throat until I began to gag and water in my eyes. I had him in my mouth balls deep and Candice was thrusting up to him with all her might. She was humping his face and chin just as hard as she could. She yanked his head down harder onto her half hairy cunt.

Candice started to come and she could hardly stop. The more she screamed the more her pussy would squirt. I saw it pop off right down my hubby's throat. Once he got a mouth full of her cunt juice his cock started to spew in my mouth. His cream was so thick and gooey and it tasted delicious. Once the two of them came, they both turned to me and got me off. Candice nursed on my big swollen tits and my husband went down and sucked my pussy lips. It felt fucking amazing having two on me at once fulfilling my every desire.

It didn't take long before I was at the back door of orgasm. While hubby ate me out Candice plunged her middle finger in my ass and the sensation of both holes being filled is what made me cream my cunt all over the place. I went nearly nuts once I began spilling my cunt juice. Hubby could hardly swallow it all and then Candice joined him for a drink. I got them both drenched before my orgasm was complete. Our first ménage was a complete success and hubby and I started doing it more often. We loved having three times the fun!

ABOUT THE AUTHOR

Kellen Prime is an emerging erotica author of many erotica kinks and sub-genres. This is Kellen's thirteenth book. Be sure to check out other books and leave a review if this story got you hot!

Visit my blog at Kellen Prime Blog

Join my newsletter for exclusive previews Kellen Prime Newsletter

Follow me on Twitter at Kellen Prime Twitter

Like my page on Facebook at Kellen Prime FB

Sign up for Free Stories from Xplicit Press Authors

Xplicit Press Author Updates

Like Xplicit Press on Facebook

Follow Xplicit Press on Twitter

Readers: I want to expand a few of the stories to see where the characters can be explored further. If there are any of the stories that you would like to read more about again, I'd love to hear from you!

Keep In Touch
KellenPrime.com
info@kellenprime.com